For my wonderful editor, Kristen —T.R.

Published in the United States by Random House Children's
Books, a division of Penguin Random House LLC,
1745 Broadway, New York, NY 10019, and in Canada by
Penguin Random House Canada Limited, Toronto,
in conjunction with Disney Enterprises, Inc.
Random House and the colophon are registered
trademarks of Penguin Random House LLC.

randomhousekids.com

ISBN 978-0-7364-3513-0 (trade)
ISBN 978-0-7364-8235-6 (lib. bdg.)

Printed in the United States of America

10 9 8 7 6 5 4 3 2 1

Random House Children's Books supports the
First Amendment and celebrates the right to read.

The Pet Pawlympics

By Tennant Redbank

Illustrated by Michela Frare and Angela Capolupo

Random House 🏠 New York

Petite the pony raced across the field behind Belle's castle. Her tail was streaming behind her. Her mane rippled in waves.

Petite's puppy friend, Teacup, was sitting on the fence, cheering her on. "Go, Petite!" Teacup called. "You're as fast as the wind!"

"Watch this!" Petite called back.

In front of her, a stream cut across one corner of the field. Petite flattened her ears and raced toward it. When it was steps away, she leaped across.

Thump, thump. Petite's hooves hit the grass on the other side. Without breaking stride, she rounded the edge of the field and headed for the fallen tree at the far end. Lifting her front legs and then her back legs, she cleared it with ease.

"Bravo!" Teacup cheered.

"One more!" Petite called. She looked around and saw a fence rail that had broken in a storm. It was higher than

the fallen tree. But Petite knew she could make it.

Petite neared the broken rail. She leaped. She soared . . . over the fence!

Petite let her pace slow to a gallop, then a trot. She came to a stop right in front of Teacup.

"That was fantastic!" Teacup said. "You're a star!"

Petite ducked her head shyly. Sure, she loved to run and jump. But Teacup was the real star at the palace. She knew all kinds of tricks. She could balance a cup on her nose. She could leap through a hoop and do fancy rolls. Though Teacup was smaller, Petite always felt she was in the puppy's shadow.

"It's nothing," Petite said. "Not like your tricks! I'm just jumping and running."

"It's not nothing!" Teacup declared. "You need to be more confident—" Her eyes widened, and she stopped speaking.

Petite followed the puppy's gaze across the field. Blown by a breeze, a glowing blue bubble floated toward them across the grass.

"Wh-what's that?" Teacup asked.

Petite knew exactly what it was. But

she didn't want to ruin the surprise for her friend.

The bubble blew closer. Teacup took a step back. The bubble seemed to follow her. It got nearer and nearer. And then it brushed against her whiskers.

Teacup wrinkled her nose. She tried to keep from sneezing, but . . .

She couldn't help herself.

"*Ahh-CHOO!*"

The sneeze blew the bubble to bits! Where the bubble had been, a glittering bird now hovered—Ms. Featherbon the hummingbird! She was Petite's friend from Whisker Haven.

Ms. Featherbon wore a dress and a hat. The hat was tied with a bow under her chin. The bird gave Petite and Teacup a funny little bow.

"Hello. My name is Ms. Featherbon," she said to Teacup. Then she turned to Petite. "Did you say something about jumping?"

Petite tilted her head. "I did," she said.

"Petite is a terrific jumper," Teacup added.

Petite blushed. She wished Teacup would stop saying that!

"Good, good," Ms. Featherbon said. "I knew I could count on you. We're having a competition in Whisker Haven today. The Pet Pawlympics, to be exact."

"The Pet Pawlympics?" Petite asked.

"Whisker Haven?" Teacup said.

"Yes, yes," Ms. Featherbon said. "Whisker Haven is a magical place where the pets of different princesses can visit each other and play together."

Teacup's eyes got big.

"It is very special," said Ms. Featherbon. "And the Pawlympics is a once-a-summer event. There will be wonderful prizes."

"Will there be . . . jumping?" Petite asked shyly.

"Of course!" Ms. Featherbon said. "Did I forget to say that? Now come along, Petite.

The others are waiting for you!"

Petite looked nervously at Teacup.

"You want us to go . . . now?"

Ms. Featherbon nodded. "Right away!
There's no time to lose!"

"I don't know," Petite said slowly. "I
like to jump. But a competition? I'm
not that good."

"Of course you are!" Teacup said.
"We'd love to go! Just let me—" She
frowned. "Oh, no. My show! I need to
perform my tricks in the village in half
an hour!"

"Can't you skip it?" Petite asked. She

didn't want to go to the competition by herself!

Teacup shook her head. "I promised," she said. "But you have to go!" She leaped onto Petite's back and whispered in her ear, "Don't worry. You'll be amazing. Win a ribbon for me, okay?"

Petite nodded. She would do anything for her friend. If Teacup wanted a ribbon, she would do her best to win one!

Teacup dropped from Petite's back to the ground.

"Good luck!" the puppy called, then headed for the village.

"Are you ready?" Ms. Featherbon asked Petite.

Petite whinnied. But *was* she ready? She wasn't so sure.

"Let's go!" Ms. Featherbon flitted across the field toward the palace. Petite

trotted after her. For such a little bird, Ms. Featherbon was fast!

The hummingbird led Petite through the palace. They stopped in front of a door in the great hall. The door was Petite's portal to Whisker Haven.

Ms. Featherbon hovered in the air above the pony. "Why so slow today?" she asked.

"I just—I'm not sure I'm a very good jumper," Petite said. She didn't want to let her friends down.

Ms. Featherbon waved a wing. "There's no need to be nervous," she said.

Petite took a deep breath. With a swish of her tail, she jumped through the portal into Whisker Haven.

She was worried about the competition, but she was also happy to be back in one of her favorite places!

Petite stepped into the great hall of the Whisker Haven Pawlace. Her Whisker Haven friends usually came running over as soon as she arrived. But today the great hall was quiet.

"We're out here, Ms. Featherbon!" a bright orange cat called from the front doors of the Pawlace. It was Petite's friend Treasure. She led Petite and

Ms. Featherbon to a nearby tree. Petite said hello to Treasure and a few other friends—a bunny named Berry, a tiger named Sultan, and a puppy named Pumpkin.

There was also an orange-striped kitten Petite had never seen before. He was wearing a cap, a vest, and a little red bow tie.

"Welcome to the Pet Pawlympics!" said the kitten, taking off his cap. "My name is Barnaby Pickles. I'll be the host of today's games. Is everybody ready for the toughest, trickiest competition ever?"

"Umm . . . ," replied Petite.

"We always ask a Critterzen to host the games," said Ms. Featherbon, referring to the animals who lived in the village. She looked around. "Now, where's Dreamy?"

"Aha!" She flitted over to a pink kitten dozing on the grass. "Asleep again." She poked the kitten with her beak. "Wake up, Dreamy!"

The kitten opened one eye. "Oh, but I

was having the loveliest dream," she said with a yawn.

"You can sleep later," Ms. Featherbon said. "It's time for the Pawlympics to begin! Barnaby, what is the first event?"

"Jumping!" said the cat. "Except first you have to figure out what you'll be jumping over. Start searching, everyone!"

A loud cheer came from a nearby grandstand set up next to the tree. The seats were filled with other Critterzens. Miss Sophia the sloth was there, and so were Lucy the puppy, Tillie the kitten, and more!

"The Critterzens are here to watch the Pawlympics," Berry said.

"The Pawlympics is a big deal," Pumpkin added.

Petite felt a lump in her throat. She hadn't known the Pet Pawlympics would have an audience!

"Sultan will start!" called Barnaby Pickles. "Good luck—you'll need it!"

Sultan looked around and found a large rock near the edge of the meadow. "That must be it!" he said. He took a running start and leaped over the rock.

"Nice jump!" Barnaby called. "But

that's not it!" He burst into laughter.

Sultan frowned.

"I know!" Berry said. "It's this bush." Her tail twitched, and she hopped over a rosebush.

"Wrong again!" Barnaby replied. "But nice hop, Berry!"

Treasure pointed a paw at a tree on the edge of the meadow. "I know!" she said. "It's a high jump! We have to jump over that branch!"

A long branch stuck straight out from the tree, parallel to the ground.

"Treasure is correct!" Barnaby called.

"Whoever jumps over that branch gets the ribbon."

Petite felt the lump in her throat grow bigger. A high jump? She didn't know if she could jump high!

Treasure stood on the ground under the branch. "Here goes!" she said. Treasure

jumped as high as she could. But it wasn't high enough.

Treasure laughed. "Oh, well," she said with a shrug. "No ribbon for me!"

Sultan tried next. He jumped, but he didn't go over the branch. Instead he dug his claws into the trunk and began to climb the tree.

"Sultan? Where are you going?" Ms. Featherbon called. Sultan ignored her and continued climbing.

Ms. Featherbon sighed. "Oh, dear."

"You're up next, Dreamy," said Barnaby Pickles. But there was no answer.

"Dreamy?" he repeated.

"Dreamy is napping," Pumpkin said.

"Maybe Petite can go."

"Oh no, that's okay," Petite said. "You go!"

"I'll go!" Berry said. She backed up. She bounced on her bunny feet once, twice, three times. Then, with a mighty leap, she jumped up, up, up—and over the branch. She landed lightly on the other side!

The pets and the Critterzens cheered loudly.

"That's how it's done!" Pumpkin said.

"I can do it, too. I know I can!" Like Berry,

Pumpkin bounced once, twice, three times on her paws. Then she jumped up . . .

. . . and landed on the branch!

"I told you this was tough!" Barnaby said. "Okay, jump down."

But Pumpkin was scared. She wrapped her paws around the branch. Her tail drooped, and she shook her head. "Jump down? Are you kidding?" she said. "Can't you see how far away the ground is?"

"Come on, Pumpkin," Treasure called. "Jump down!"

Sultan poked his head out from the

leaves on a higher branch. "Or come up!"

he invited.

"Nope, nope, nope," Pumpkin said,

clinging to the branch. "I'll just stay here.

You start the next event instead."

"Petite, you're good at jumping," Ms.

Featherbon said. "Can you get her down?"

"I'll try," Petite said. She backed up

and raced toward the branch. But even

before she got there, she knew her footing

was off. She took a long stride, then a half

stride, and jumped. She flew upward, but

her hooves knocked against the branch

and she came right back down again.

Darn! She had totally mistimed her leap. High-jumping wasn't easy!

Petite blew her mane out of her eyes and looked up at the tree. Poor Pumpkin! She was still stuck. Petite really wanted to help. Maybe she couldn't jump high, but . . . she was taller than the other pets.

Petite put her hooves on the trunk. She

stretched her neck toward the branches.

"Pumpkin," she called, "you don't have to jump all the way down. Just to my head, okay?"

Pumpkin opened one eye and looked at Petite. "Nope, nope, nope, nope. . . . Well, okay . . . maybe I can do that," she said. "I think." She inched her way along the branch. Then she slid down the trunk. . . .

Thunk! The puppy landed on Petite's head.

She was heavier than she looked! Petite lowered her head, and Pumpkin slid off into the grass.

"Well, that was very exciting!" Ms. Featherbon said. "You all did royally wonderful!" She glanced over at Dreamy, and the sleeping kitten let out a light snore.

"But there is only one ribbon," said Barnaby Pickles. "It goes to . . . Berry!"

Berry hopped up and down as Barnaby tied a frilly blue ribbon around her neck.

The Critterzens clapped. The pets cheered. Petite stomped her feet in appreciation. Berry had done a great job!

"Better luck next time, pony," said Barnaby Pickles. He winked at Petite.

Sure, Petite wished she had done better, too. She really wanted to win a ribbon for Teacup. Maybe she'd be better at the next Pet Pawlympics event.

"Jumping didn't go quite as planned," Ms. Featherbon said.

"But wait until you hear what's next," said Barnaby Pickles. "Boat races!"

Boat races? Petite had never been in a boat before. This was going to be interesting!

Barnaby Pickles and Ms. Featherbon led the pets to the bay, where six sailboats were tied to the dock. The Critterzens were lined up along the edge of the water. One of them held up a banner that said GO, PETS!

"Everyone pick a sailboat!" Barnaby Pickles called. "And don't forget your life jackets!" He added. "You'll need them."

Except for the color of the sails, all the boats looked the same to Petite.

Treasure went straight for the boat with the blue sail. Pumpkin picked the one with the red sail, and Sultan took the yellow one. Dreamy's was white.

Two boats were left. One had a green sail, and one had an orange sail.

"Which do you want, Petite?" Berry asked.

"You pick," Petite said. "I'm not much of a sailor."

Berry twitched her nose. "Me neither! But okay, I'll take the green one."

Petite nodded. "Good luck, Berry," she said. "I hope you win!"

She meant it. Berry had been so happy when she won the jumping event. It would be nice if she could win again. Actually, Petite wished all her friends could win.

Petite leaped onto the boat, and it rocked slightly under her hooves. She found the tiller, which she had seen sailors use to steer a boat.

"All right!" Barnaby Pickles called. "Cast off on three. One. Two. Three!"

As the pets untied their ropes, all the sails began flapping wildly. They weren't tied down!

"Whoa!" cried Petite. She rushed to tie her sail in place. She could see the other pets doing the same.

On the dock, Barnaby Pickles was doubled over with laughter.

"That's not funny, Barnaby Pickles!" Berry shouted.

Soon all the boats were sailing smoothly away from the dock. They were off!

Petite's tail streamed behind her. Her mane rippled in the wind. She closed her eyes and felt the breeze on her face. It was just like running!

When she opened her eyes, she was surprised to see that her boat was doing well. Treasure was in the lead, but Petite was in second place!

She nosed the tiller slightly to get more wind in her sail, and her boat jumped ahead.

This is fun! she thought.

She looked behind her. The other boats were strung out in a line. Well, except for Dreamy's. It went in circles while Dreamy napped in the bow.

Then the boat with the green sail heaved to one side, its sail tilting at a sharp angle. Petite heard a soft "Oh!" and a splash. She saw something fall off the side of the boat.

That something was Berry!

Petite pushed her sailboat's tiller with both hooves, and it made a sharp turn.

Treasure shot past her. "Come back!" she called. "You're going the wrong way!"

But Petite sailed her boat back to Berry's boat. Berry bobbed in the water like a furry little cork.

"Darn cottontail!" Berry said. "It's waterlogged. I can't pull myself up."

"I'll help," Petite said. She took the back of Berry's life jacket into her mouth. After giving the bunny a gentle shake to get the water off, she dropped Berry into her own boat.

"Thanks for stopping, Petite," Berry said. "You could have had a ribbon!"

"That's okay," Petite said.

Berry and Petite sailed to the other end

of the bay, where Barnaby was pinning a blue ribbon to Treasure's collar.

"Don't worry," Ms. Featherbon said. "We have one more event." She looked at Petite and smiled.

"Running!" Barnaby announced.

The pets gathered at the starting line. The meadow stretched out before them, soft green grass with pretty pink and yellow wildflowers. Several Critterzens had spread out blankets next to the meadow. A round white kitten named Mr. Chow was passing out kibble treats to all his friends.

"Normally we'd run on the track," Ms.

Featherbon explained. "But some sea turtles chose it for their nesting grounds. We didn't want to bother them."

"The meadow is even better," said Barnaby Pickles. "Just follow the signs." He pointed to a piece of wood with an arrow painted on it. Several more signs were scattered across the meadow.

Petite lifted her nose higher. Track or meadow—it didn't matter to her. She couldn't wait to begin!

"Is everyone ready?" Barnaby Pickles asked. The participants nodded.

"Follow the signs to the far fence and

back. First one to cross this line again wins," Barnaby called. "Okay . . . go!"

The pets took off. Sultan was very fast, and so was Pumpkin. Each of Berry's jumps took her surprisingly far. Treasure had a natural quickness. Petite didn't see Dreamy anywhere. She was probably napping again.

Suddenly—*oomph!* Petite bumped right into Sultan.

Crash! Treasure collided with Berry. The signs were all mixed up. They were making the pets cross paths and bump into each other!

At the starting line, Barnaby was giggling.

"Barnaby Pickles!" Ms. Featherbon scolded. "Pets, please ignore the signs. To the far fence and back—no turns!"

Petite found her stride, and her hooves flew across the meadow. The wind tugged at her mane and tail. She tossed her head back and forth. It felt wonderful to be running again!

Petite was in the lead. Maybe she would win this event! Then she could take a ribbon back to Teacup, as she'd promised.

Petite reached the far fence first. She turned and raced back.

Just then, a little "Meow!" reached her ears. She heard a soft "Help?"

Petite slowed her pace. She looked in every direction but didn't see anyone. She swiveled her ears, listening for the sound again.

There it was.

"Help!"

It sounded like Treasure!

Petite ran toward the cry. "Treasure?" she called.

"Down here!"

Petite looked down. At her feet was a deep hole. A groundhog hole.

Sultan ran past, and immediately came back. "What are you doing?" he asked Petite.

"I think Treasure has fallen into that hole!" she explained, looking worried.

Petite and Sultan looked into the dark hole. Petite thought she could make out the glimmer of cat eyes at the bottom.

A minute later, Pumpkin and Berry approached. They stopped when they saw Petite and Sultan.

"What are you looking at?" Berry asked.

"Treasure," Sultan answered. "She's down in the hole!"

"We have to get her out!" Pumpkin said.

Petite nodded. Her new friend was in trouble. She was sure the pets could figure out a way to help together. "Okay, what we need is a vine—"

"I'll get it!" Sultan cried. He raced off into the woods.

"I can pull her up. She's not very heavy," Petite said, just as Sultan returned with a very long vine.

Pumpkin looped the vine around Petite's middle and pulled it tight. Berry dropped the other end down into the hole.

"Grab the vine!" Pumpkin called to Treasure. "Petite will pull you up!"

Petite planted her hooves in the meadow grass. She took a step away from the hole, then another and another. With each step, Treasure was lifted farther up. Finally, she popped right out of the hole!

"Whew!" Treasure said. "Thanks for saving me. I tried to climb out, but the dirt walls kept crumbling." She shook some dirt from her tail. "*Me-wow,* that was an adventure!"

Treasure rode on Petite's back to the finish line. Ms. Featherbon and Barnaby Pickles were waiting for them. When Ms. Featherbon saw them, she smiled.

"There you are!" she said.

"We had to stop to help Treasure," Sultan said. "She fell into a hole."

"Petite rescued her!" Berry added.

Petite ducked her head. It was no big deal. Any pet would have done the same.

"I guess no one won," Pumpkin said.

"Someone did win," Barnaby said, "but you'll never guess who."

Dreamy yawned. "I don't know how it happened," she said. "I woke up, and no one was here. So I went looking. I wandered all the way to the far fence. I wandered all the way back here. The next thing I knew, Ms. Featherbon and the Critterzens were clapping and cheering for me!"

For a moment, the pets were stunned. Dreamy? *Dreamy* was the fastest pet of all? Then Petite started to laugh. Treasure giggled. Sultan snorted. Pumpkin rolled on her back, her paws in the air. Berry thumped her bunny feet.

"Hooray for Dreamy!" Petite yelled.

"Hooray! Hooray!" the other pets cheered. The Critterzens hooted, meowed, and barked.

Dreamy turned even pinker.

"I still can't believe it," Barnaby said, "but Dreamy wins the ribbon!" He pinned a blue ribbon to Dreamy's jeweled collar.

Dreamy didn't notice. She was already asleep again.

At the sight of the ribbon, Petite felt a twinge of sadness. She hadn't won a ribbon. Not for jumping. Not for sailing. Not for running. But she had had a wonderful time with her friends. She looked around at Berry, Sultan, Pumpkin,

Treasure, Dreamy, Ms. Featherbon, and Barnaby Pickles, and smiled.

"But wait! Silly me, I almost forgot. Barnaby has one more award to give out!" Ms. Featherbon said. She held up another ribbon. This one wasn't blue. It was a lovely, sparkly gold.

"This ribbon isn't for the fastest runner or the highest jumper or the best sailor," Ms. Featherbon said. "It's for something more important. It's for the best friend. Go ahead, Barnaby. No tricks this time."

"The ribbon goes to . . . Petite!"

Petite lifted her head. "Me?" she said.

"How can I be the best friend?"

"You helped me when I was stuck in the tree," Pumpkin said.

"You rescued me from the water," Berry said.

"You pulled me out of the hole," Treasure said.

"It's no contest," Ms. Featherbon said.

"Petite, you are a gold-ribbon friend," Barnaby said. He pinned the ribbon to Petite's halter.

Petite hid behind her mane. She was beaming. What an amazing day! She'd jumped high. She'd sailed with a breeze. She'd run like the wind. Most of all, she'd made memories with her friends.

Petite couldn't wait to tell Teacup. And she couldn't wait to give Teacup the sparkly ribbon.

Petite really *was* a gold-ribbon friend!